Native American Biographies

CHIEF JOSEPH

Rachel A. Koestler-Grack

Heinemann Library
Chicago, Illinois

Designed by Kim Saar/Heinemann Library
Maps by John Fleck
Photo research by Alan Gottlieb
Printed in China by WKT Company Limited

08 07 06 05 04
10 9 8 7 6 5 4 3 2 1

Library of Congress Cataloging-in-Publication Data
Koestler-Grack, Rachel A., 1973-
  Chief Joseph / Rachel A. Koestler-Grack.
    p. cm. -- (Native American biographies)
  Summary: A biography of Chief Joseph, leader of the Nez Perce people in the late 1800s, including his childhood, the battles his tribe fought in hopes of remaining on their land, and their eventual removal to reservations.
  Includes bibliographical references and index.
  ISBN 1-4034-5001-3 (lib. bdg.) -- ISBN 1-4034-5008-0 (pbk.)
  1. Joseph, Nez Perc,e Chief, 1840-1904--Juvenile literature. 2. Nez Perc,e Indians--Kings and rulers--Biography--Juvenile literature. 3. Nez Perc,e Indians--Wars, 1877--Juvenile literature. 4. Nez Perc,e Indians--Relocation--Juvenile literature. 5. Forced migration--Oregon--Wallowa River Valley--Juvenile literature. [1. Joseph, Nez Perc,e Chief, 1840-1904. 2. Nez Perc,e Indians--Biography. 3. Indians of North America--Northwest, Pacific--Biography. 4. Kings, queens, rulers, etc.] I. Title. II. Series: Native American biographies (Heinemann Library (Firm))
  E99.N5J5865 2004
  979.5004'974124'0092--dc22

2003020488

Acknowledgments
The author and publisher are grateful to the following for permission to reproduce copyright material:
p. 4 The Image Bank/Getty Images; p. 5 MSCUA/University of Washington Libraries/Neg. #NA189; p. 7 Idaho State Historical Society/Neg. #684; p. 8 W. Perry Conway/Corbis; p. 9 MSCUA/University of Washington Libraries/Neg. #NA1009; p. 10 MSCUA/University of Washington Libraries/Neg. #NA941; pp. 11, 24 Washington State University Library; pp. 12, 15 Marilyn "Angel" Wynn/NativeStock; p. 13 Gary Braasch/Corbis; p. 14 National Anthropological Archives/Smithsonian Institution/Neg. #NAA-2792; pp. 16, 17 Washington State Historical Society, Tacoma; p. 18 Montana Historical Society; p. 20 MSCUA/University of Washington Libraries/Neg. #947; p. 22 Northwest Museum of Arts & Culture, Spokane, WA.; p. 23 Nez Perce National Historic Park/National Park Service; p. 25 Gilcrease Museum; p. 26 Kansas State Historical Society; p. 27 Corbis; p. 28 MSCUA/University of Washington Libraries/Neg. #NA617; p. 29 National Anthropological Archives/Smithsonian Institution/Neg. #NAA-2906

Cover photographs by (foreground) Haynes Foundation Collection/Montana Historical Society, (background) Corbis

Special thanks to Sandi McFarland for her help in the preparation of this book.

Every effort has been made to contact copyright holders of any material reproduced in this book. Any omissions will be rectified in subsequent printings if notice is given to the publisher.

The photograph of Chief Joseph on the cover of this book was taken in the 1870s. The background shows a river and mountain in Oregon.

Contents

> Some words are shown in bold, **like this.** You can find out what they mean by looking in the glossary.

Thirty Days to Move

In the spring of 1877, Chief Joseph sat on his horse looking down on the Wallowa Valley. This part of eastern Oregon was the home of his **tribe**, the Nez Perce. Years earlier, Joseph had promised his father that he would never leave Wallowa Valley. But now the United States government had given Joseph 30 days to move his people out of the valley. It made him sad to say good-bye to his **homeland**.

Part of the Wallowa Valley is protected today as a natural area. This photo shows Zumwalt Prairie Preserve, with the Wallowa Mountains in the background.

Joseph wanted to live peacefully. If the Nez Perce refused to move, it would start a war. Chief Joseph worked hard to keep his people free. He led his **band** of Nez Perce through difficult times.

Nimiipuu

French fur traders gave Chief Joseph's people the name *Nez Perce*. *Nez perce* means "pierced nose" in French. Some Nez Perce wore rings in their noses. The Nez Perce call themselves *Nimiipuu*. This means "the real people."

This photograph of Chief Joseph was taken by photographer Edward Curtis in 1903.

Young Joseph

In the summer of 1840, a Nez Perce woman gave birth to a baby boy near Joseph's Creek in present-day Oregon. Her name was Arenoth. The boy later became known as Joseph. The Nez Perce people had many different **bands.** Each band had its own village and leader. Joseph's family belonged to the Wal-lam-wat-kin band of the Nez Perce. Tuekakas, Joseph's father, was chief of the Wal-lam-wat-kin band.

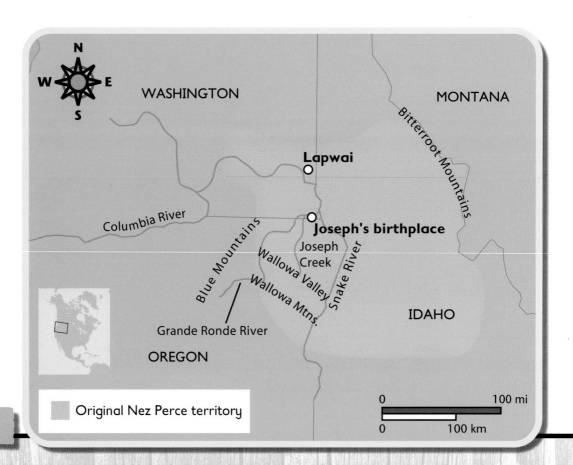

WASHINGTON

MONTANA

Bitterroot Mountains

Lapwai

Columbia River

Joseph's birthplace

Joseph Creek

Blue Mountains

Wallowa Valley

Snake River

Wallowa Mtns.

IDAHO

Grande Ronde River

OREGON

Original Nez Perce territory

0   100 mi

0   100 km

This photo shows American Indian tepees in a circle at Lapwai Mission.

Missionaries came to Nez Perce lands. Tuekakas learned about the **Christian religion** from the missionaries. The missionaries called the chief Old Joseph. His son was Young Joseph. Young Joseph spent much of his first five years at the nearby Lapwai Mission school. There, Joseph studied the English alphabet. One day, some American Indians attacked the missionaries. The Nez Perce people feared they would be blamed. Young Joseph stopped going to the school.

Tuekakas taught his son about the Nez Perce way of life. He took Young Joseph hunting for deer and elk. He showed Young Joseph how to catch salmon in nearby streams. Tuekakas taught his son how to make knives, arrows, and spears out of mountain goat horns and hard rocks.

The elk was one animal that young Nez Perce boys learned to hunt.

This photograph from the late 1800s shows a Nez Perce boy riding a horse. The boy's father and mother are on the right.

Young Joseph worked hard to please his father. He quickly learned how to ride a pony without a saddle. He listened carefully to the sounds of birds and other animals. He learned to **imitate** these sounds. This talent helped Joseph get close to the animals he was hunting.

These two Nez Perce boys were photographed around 1903. They are wearing ceremonial clothing.

Young Joseph learned to be giving and kind to others. He learned that it was important to share food with the poor and weak. He also learned that he should only kill animals when he needed food. Joseph lived in a large family. In the Nez Perce **culture**, men often married more than one woman. Tuekakas had several wives. Joseph had seven brothers and sisters.

Joseph's mother had another son named Ollokot. Joseph was close to his brother. The two boys had different **personalities.** Ollokot was bold and adventurous. Joseph was quiet and gentle.

Timeline

Lapwai mission was built	Young Joseph was born
1831	1840

A Nez Perce Story

Wise Coyote stabbed an evil monster in the heart. He cut the monster into many pieces. Coyote used the pieces to form the different **tribes.** Then he squeezed blood from the monster's heart. He made this blood into the Nez Perce people.

Ollokot became a strong warrior. He grew to be over six feet tall.

Thunder over the Mountains

When Joseph was nine years old, a Nez Perce **holy man** began teaching him. In Nez Perce **culture**, each child has a **guardian spirit** called *Wyakin*. Joseph's teacher helped him find his *Wyakin*. Joseph's teacher prepared him for a **vision quest**.

*Nez Perce children learned many things by listening to their **elders**.*

Early one spring morning, Young Joseph left his family's tepee and walked out of the village. He walked for several hours. Finally, he came to a steep rock ridge. He climbed to the top and sat down cross-legged. He waited for his *Wyakin*. Hours went by. Young Joseph was hungry, but he knew he must not eat. Soon the sun went down. Young Joseph shivered in the cold.

On his vision quest, Young Joseph climbed up a mountain like this one near the Wallowa Valley.

Every Nez Perce boy goes through a vision quest. This photograph was taken in the late 1800s or early 1900s.

Finally the sun rose. Joseph's tongue and throat were dry. He needed a drink of cold water. His body felt weak with hunger and he fell asleep. While he slept, *Wyakin* sent Young Joseph a dream. When Joseph woke up, he knew that his name had been chosen. He got up and walked home.

The following spring Young Joseph joined in the *Wee'kwetset* **ceremony.** In this special event, Young Joseph would reveal his name. The entire village gathered in the dance lodge. Villagers began to dance around the fires. Young Joseph sang the words that his *Wyakin* had taught him. He sang his name, *In-mut-too-yah-lat-lat.* This means "Thunder traveling over the mountains."

Today Nez Perce children dance in ceremonies such as **powwows.** These children are dancing at a powwow in Wallowa Valley.

Learning to Be a Chief

When Joseph was fifteen, he traveled with his father to Walla Walla in present-day Oregon. Here, Tuekakas met with leaders from the United States government. They wanted to buy part of the Nez Perce land for **settlers**. Both sides signed a **treaty**. The Nez Perce sold a small part of their land to the settlers. But the Nez Perce kept most of their land, including Wallowa Valley.

The Nez Perce would ride into treaty council on horseback. United States Army soldier Gustavus Sohon made this drawing at the Walla Walla council in 1855.

This drawing of Old Joseph was also made by Gustavus Sohon during the 1855 treaty council.

As Joseph grew older, more settlers came to Nez Perce lands. Some of them built homes there. Tuekakas believed the settlers were disobeying the treaty. When Joseph was 23, some settlers wanted to buy more land. Young Joseph and his brother, Ollokot, went with their father to the meeting. Tuekakas and many other Nez Perce chiefs refused to sell their land.

Some Nez Perce chiefs at the meeting thought that selling the land was a good idea. These chiefs did not live in Wallowa Valley. They signed a **treaty** with the United States government. This agreement gave away the land in Wallowa Valley. Many groups of Nez Perce people called this the "thief" treaty. Joseph and other Nez Perce chiefs did not sign the treaty. They believed they would stay in their **homeland**.

In Their Own Words

"Our fathers gave us many laws, which they had learned from their fathers. These laws were good. They told us to treat all men as they treated us…that it was a disgrace to tell a lie."

—Chief Joseph
1879

In 1871 Tuekakas became very sick. Tuekakas spoke slowly to his son:

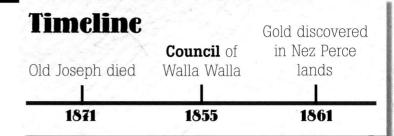

"My son, you are the chief of these people now. This land holds the bones of our fathers and mothers. Do not give it away." Then Tuekakas died. Joseph buried him in Wallowa Valley. Young Joseph became chief. He believed it was better to solve problems without fighting. But soon he would have to struggle to keep his people free.

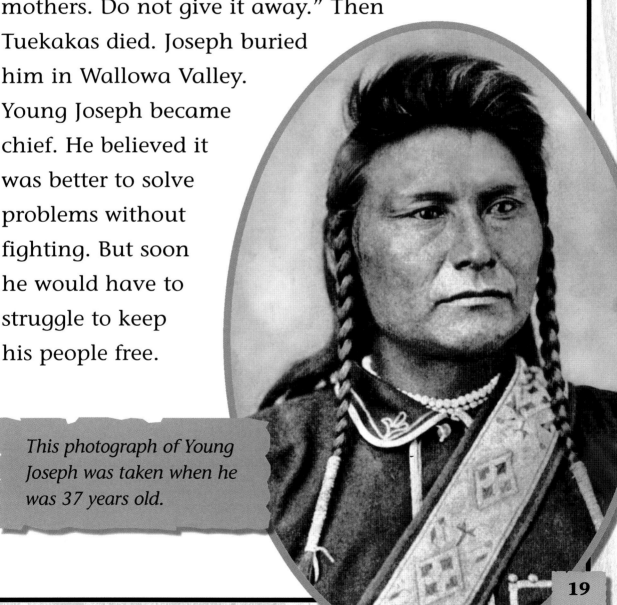

This photograph of Young Joseph was taken when he was 37 years old.

19

Flight for Freedom

Joseph's people continued to have problems with white **settlers** in the Wallowa Valley. Settlers believed they had a right to live on Nez Perce land. Joseph's people believed they still owned their **homeland.** Sometimes there was fighting between the settlers and the Nez Perce. Chief Joseph still hoped for peace. On May 14, 1877, Joseph agreed to move his **band** to the Lapwai **Reservation.** He thought his people could someday return to the Wallowa Valley.

After a while Joseph's band of the Nez Perce had to leave Wallowa Valley.

On the way to Lapwai, fighting broke out between Joseph's people and United States soldiers. Joseph knew it would be difficult to avoid a war. His band crossed the Salmon River. Joseph knew the soldiers would have a more difficult time crossing the river than his people. Joseph planned to cross the plains quickly. There, he hoped to live in freedom.

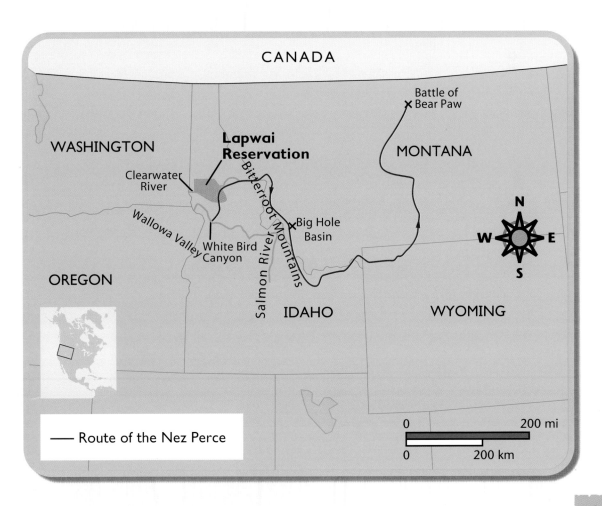

This photograph of Chief Joseph's band of the Nez Perce was taken in 1877.

United States soldiers made surprise attacks on the Nez Perce camp. Chief Joseph did not want to fight. But he had to protect his people. The Nez Perce continued on their trail. Another group of soldiers began following them. Joseph realized that his people would never be free in the United States. Their only hope was to escape to Canada.

In Their Own Words

"When my young men began the killing, my heart was hurt."
—Chief Joseph

On August 8th, the Nez Perce camped near the Big Hole

Timeline

Joseph agreed to move his people to Lapwai	Fighting began	Battle of Big Hole
May 14, 1877	**June 1877**	**August 8, 1877**

Basin in present-day Montana. They thought the soldiers were several days behind them. But early the next morning, soldiers attacked the camp. Nez Perce **warriors** grabbed for their guns. After two days of battle, the soldiers **retreated.** But about 90 Nez Perce people had died, including Joseph's wife. Joseph was deeply hurt by her death.

The place where the Battle of Big Hole took place is now a national monument.

Fight No More

On September 29, 1877, the Nez Perce were only 40 miles (65 kilometers) from Canada. The next morning soldiers charged the camp. The Nez Perce **warriors** fought hard. But there were too few of them. Soliders killed Ollokot during the battle. All Joseph had ever wanted was peace. He could not bring death to his people any longer. On October 5th, Chief Joseph **surrendered.** After 1,700 miles (2,700 kilometers) of running, the war was over.

The Nez Perce warrior and artist Peopeo Tholekt drew this picture of the Battle of Bear Paw. This was the last battle before Joseph surrendered to the United States Army.

Before Chief Joseph surrendered, he had lost almost 250 of his people at the Battle of Bear Paw. The United States Army had lost almost the same number of soldiers.

Joseph's people had to give up their freedom. But Joseph did not give up. He kept asking the United States government to let his people return to Wallowa Valley. The government forced them to live on a faraway **reservation** in Kansas.

In Their Own Words

"I am tired. My heart is sick and sad. . . I will fight no more forever."

—Chief Joseph
at his surrender

*Chief Joseph's people were sent to Fort Leavenworth in Kansas. It was a very different place from their **homeland.***

Chief Joseph and his people arrived at the **reservation** in Kansas on November 27, 1877. Their new homes were near a swamp. Many Nez Perce caught **malaria** and died, including Joseph's two-year-old daughter. Joseph traveled to Washington, D.C., and spoke to the president. Joseph reminded him that the Nez Perce had never sold their land. But his talks did not help.

In 1885 Joseph and some Nez Perce moved to a reservation

Timeline

Chief Joseph **surrendered**	Nez Perce arrived to Fort Leavenworth in Kansas	Some Nez Perce moved to a reservation in Nespelem, Washington
October 5, 1877	November 1877	1885

in Nespelem, Washington. When Joseph was 49, he visited Wallowa Valley. He offered to buy some land for his people. But **settlers** refused to sell it. On September 21, 1904, Joseph died. He was 64 years old. The reservation doctor told the people that Joseph died of a broken heart. The Nez Perce mourned the loss of their great chief.

After being moved from place to place, some Nez Perce boarded a train that would take them to the Colville Reservation in Washington.

The Great Chief

In 1905 a friend of Chief Joseph built a monument at his grave at Nespelem. Later, some Nez Perce people wanted to honor Chief Joseph. They helped create the Chief Joseph Memorial and Historical Association. This group has worked hard to teach others about Joseph's love for his people and his **homeland**.

The Chief Joseph Monument was finished in 1905. A Nez Perce man named Yellow Bull spoke at the dedication ceremony. He said, "Joseph is dead, but his words will live forever."

Today people remember Chief Joseph's courage. He led his people on a 1,700-mile (2,700-kilometer) trip for freedom. Joseph's struggle for peace brought hope to the Nez Perce. His words and actions have helped many people understand the Nez Perce way of life.

In 1879 Chief Joseph said, "Whenever the white man treats the Indian as they treat each other, then we shall have no more wars."

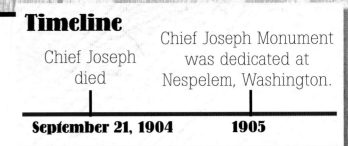

Timeline

Chief Joseph died	Chief Joseph Monument was dedicated at Nespelem, Washington.
September 21, 1904	1905

29

Glossary

band   group of people

basin   land that is drained by a river

ceremony   event that celebrates a
   special occasion

Christian   based on the teachings of Jesus Christ

council   group of leaders who make decisions for
   a group of people

culture   way of life of a group of people

dedication   opening a new building or monument

elder   older person, such as a grandparent, who is
   treated with respect

guardian spirit   invisible force or being that
   protects a person from harm

holy man   person with spiritual or religious power

homeland   place that a group of people
   comes from

imitate   look or sound like something else

malaria   serious disease common in hot, wet areas

missionary   person who teaches others about his or her religion

personality   way a person acts or behaves

powwow   American Indian gathering or celebration

religion   system of spiritual beliefs and practices

reservation   land kept by Indians when they signed treaties

retreat   run away from a battle

settler   person who makes a home in a new place

surrender   give up

treaty   agreement between governments or groups of people

tribe   group of people who share language, customs, beliefs, and often government

vision quest   religious experience in which a person has a special dream

warrior   person who fights in battles

More Books to Read

Carpenter, Jack and Diane Shaughnessy. *Chief Joseph: Nez Perce Peacekeeper.* New York: Powerkids Press, 1998.

Englar, Mary. *Chief Joseph.* Minnetonka, Minn.: Capstone Press, 2004.

Takacs, Stephanie. *The Nez Perce.* Danbury, Conn.: Scholastic Library, 2003.

Index